WILL & PA'S
new friend

by Lucy Kincaid
Illustrated by Eric Kincaid

Brimax Books · Newmarket · England

A Red Ear

It was early morning. Specks of sawdust were floating up into the shaft of sunlight coming through the window. Pa put down his saw and stretched his aching back.

"Have you found it?" he called, looking towards a corner where there seemed to be nothing but shadows.

There was a slither and the sound of something sliding. Something fell with a bonk.

"Oh bother," said an invisible someone.

"Have you found it?" asked Pa again, as Will, draped all about with cobwebs, emerged like a ghost from the shadows.

"Not yet," said Will. He was looking for a special piece of wood which he had been saving to make a

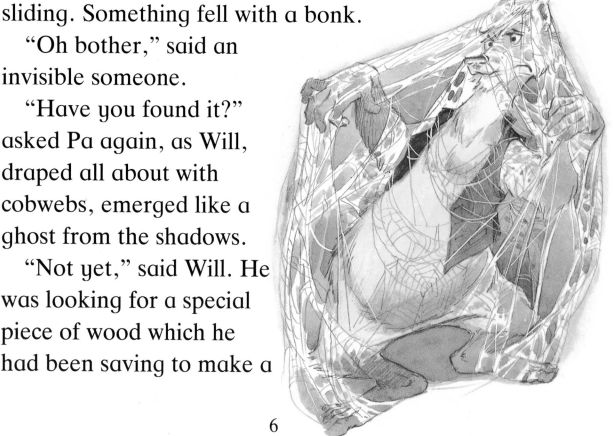

special bowl. He had put it somewhere safe and now he couldn't remember where that somewhere safe was. "I have looked everywhere," he sighed.

There was a shelf high under the eaves. Things were put there when they were no longer any use, but too good to throw away. Will began to feel his way along the shelf. He couldn't quite see what he was doing so he stood on his tiptoes. And up there, on his tiptoes, he saw something he wasn't expecting to see. He froze like a statue.

"Pa, come here," he whispered quietly, hardly daring to move his lips.

"What is it, Will?" asked Pa.

"Look there," whispered Will. He was still on tiptoe. He was still holding onto the shelf. He didn't dare let go. The only way he could point was with his nose. Pa stood on HIS tiptoes and looked over Will's shoulder. It was the only way he could see where Will's nose was pointing.

"What is it?" asked Will, trying hard not to wobble. Pa thought he could see two eyes and something fluffy.

"Perhaps it's a mouse with a beard," he said. The little eyes blinked. The something fluffy, whatever it was, brushed against Will's face. Will was so surprised he let go of the shelf and stepped backwards.

"Ow!" cried Pa, as Will stepped back onto his toes.

"That was a silly thing to do," said Pa as they both fell into a heap on the floor.

"There it goes!" cried Will.

Something small had leapt from the shelf onto the long planks in the roof and vanished.

"I'll get it down, whatever it is," said Will, already halfway up the ladder.

"Do be careful," said Pa. "It might bite."

Will came down the ladder, much faster than he had gone up it.

"Don't let it go away before I get back," he said and went up the steps to the loft. When he came back he looked like a knight in knitted armour. He was wearing an extra thick woollen jumper that reached down to his knees, a thick woollen hat pulled over his ears, a thick woollen scarf tied round his face, thick woollen socks that reached up to his knees, and thick woollen gloves.

"It won't bite me now," he said.

"It couldn't, if it tried," said Pa.

Will squeezed himself into the space between the planks and the roof. Dust started to fall. Pa waited anxiously for something to happen. Suddenly there was a shriek.

"Save me!" cried a voice Pa had never heard before. Something small, with a long tail, launched itself from the planks like a rocket and landed on Pa's shoulder.

"What have you done with Will?" demanded Pa, trying to shake the animal off. He couldn't. It was holding onto his ear as though it would never, ever, let go.

"I haven't done anything . . . there's a monster up there!"

Will's face appeared at the top of the ladder. The animal gave a frightened gasp. It buried its face in its fluffy tail and clung even tighter to Pa's ear.

"Ouch!" said Pa. He could feel his ear going red.

"It got away," said Will.

"No, it didn't. I've got it here," said Pa. "Or perhaps it would be truer to say it has got me."

Pa tried to loosen the tiny paws. He couldn't.

10

"Would you mind not
holding so tightly," he said.
Will started to peel
off his woollen armour.
"I'm not surprised it
thought you were a
monster, dressed like that,"
said Pa. "I might have
been frightened myself if I
had seen you in the dark."

"What is it?" asked Will, looking at the animal
closely, but not daring to touch it.

The fluffy tail stopped quivering. Will could see
two little eyes peeping through it. The tail moved.
Will saw whiskers and a little face with black cheeks.
Whatever it was, it was just a baby.

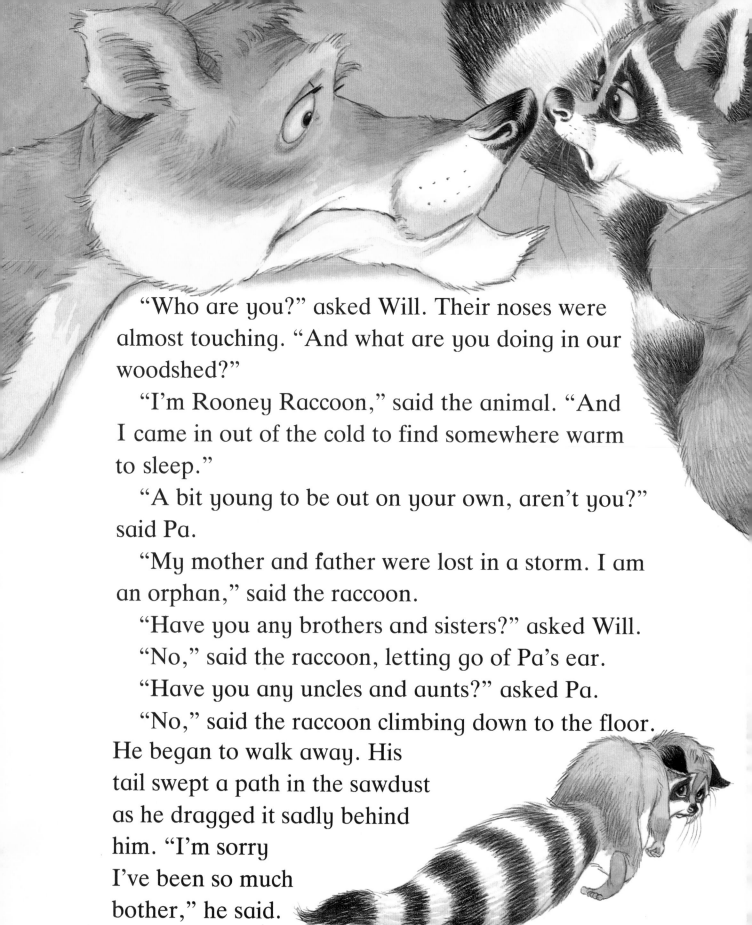

"Who are you?" asked Will. Their noses were almost touching. "And what are you doing in our woodshed?"

"I'm Rooney Raccoon," said the animal. "And I came in out of the cold to find somewhere warm to sleep."

"A bit young to be out on your own, aren't you?" said Pa.

"My mother and father were lost in a storm. I am an orphan," said the raccoon.

"Have you any brothers and sisters?" asked Will.

"No," said the raccoon, letting go of Pa's ear.

"Have you any uncles and aunts?" asked Pa.

"No," said the raccoon climbing down to the floor. He began to walk away. His tail swept a path in the sawdust as he dragged it sadly behind him. "I'm sorry I've been so much bother," he said. "I'll go now."

Pa looked at Will and Will looked at Pa.

"He's very small," said Will.

"He's very small," agreed Pa.

"I AM very small," whispered the raccoon, walking even slower. "I am very, very small."

"You are far too small to wander about on your own," said Pa. "You need looking after. You can stay here with us."

Pa picked up the raccoon and put him on Will's shoulder.

"Ouch!" said Will as the raccoon caught hold of HIS ear. "Who would have thought such a little thing could hold on so tightly."

"Or have such a big smile," said Pa.

And that was how Rooney Raccoon came to live in the woodshed with Will and his Pa, and how Will and Pa always had at least one red ear between them.

13

Hatpins

Next morning Rooney was up bright and early and eager to help.

"What shall I do?" he asked, as he danced round Pa's feet. It always took Pa a long time to wake up in the morning.

"Anything," he yawned, trying not to step on Rooney, or his tail. "Anything, as long as it keeps you away from my feet."

Rooney looked at all the sawdust lying on the floor. "Shall I sweep?" he asked.

"If you really want to," said Pa. "There is a broom in the corner."

"Don't need a broom," said Rooney. "I've got a tail."

When Will came into the woodshed, just a few minutes later, he couldn't believe his eyes. There was sawdust blowing about in clouds wherever he looked. Pa was leaning against the bench with his coat on.

At least, Will thought it was his coat until he sneezed. Then the coat lifted into the air, hovered,

and settled back to fit snuggly again. It wasn't a coat at all. It was a layer of sawdust.

"What happened?" asked Will.

Pa pointed towards a small wind that was whirling round the woodshed.

"That's what happened," sighed Pa, "And I only fell asleep for a minute."

It was Rooney, chasing sawdust with his tail.

It took all morning for the dust to settle properly. It took even longer to brush the sawdust from Pa's fur, and comb it out of his whiskers and eyebrows. It had to be done properly because they were going to tea with Aunt Tilda that afternoon.

Aunt Tilda was Pa's sister and lived in the village.

"We have brought a friend to see you," said Pa, when Aunt Tilda opened the door.

Aunt Tilda looked down her long nose and inspected Rooney from the tip of his tail to the tip of his nose.

"Is he on his best behaviour?" she asked.

"Oh yes," said Pa, though he had no idea what best behaviour in a raccoon might be.

"If he is on his best behaviour he can come in," said Aunt Tilda. She set great store by best behaviour.

They hadn't been there long when there was a knock at the door.

"That will be Millie and Mollie," said Aunt Tilda.

Millie and Mollie were friends of Aunt Tilda's. They were as alike as two peas in a pod. They were as neat and as tidy as two pins in a pin box. They were never ruffled and never looked untidy.

They let Pa take their coats and their gloves, but they kept their hats firmly on their heads. They kept all their hair tucked inside their hats. They wore them absolutely straight and pinned them to their hair with long hat pins. They never seemed to take them off. Pa often wondered if they went to bed in them.

"Good afternoon," they said, each one in turn. They looked down at Rooney.

Rooney looked up at them. They seemed very tall to him. He seemed very small to them.

They folded themselves in half like two pieces of ribbon and patted Rooney's head. He went bright pink and tried to hide behind his tail.

"Oh, how sweet," said Millie. "He's shy."

"What a lovely shade of pink," said Mollie.

They couldn't resist tickling him. It was a mistake. To begin with Rooney didn't like being tickled. It made him laugh, it was true, but he didn't like it. And for another thing, it made his tail flick. He didn't mean it to happen. It just did, whether he wanted it to or not.

"Oh my," giggled Millie as Rooney's tail flicked through her dangling beads and tickled her under the chin.

"Oh my," giggled Mollie as Rooney's tail flicked the other way and did the same to her chin.

Rooney panicked. He tried to send a message to his tail but it wouldn't listen. It did what it wanted to.

The more it flicked the more tangled it got with the strings of beads. The more tangled the beads got the closer together they pulled Millie and Mollie.

Their hats collided. Their heads bumped. Their hatpins clashed and locked together like antlers.

What a pickle they were in! There they were, nose touching nose . . . bent double like bookends facing the wrong way . . . hatpins locked like antlers . . . and their beads and Rooney's tail tied together in one big knot under their chins.

They were giggling and gasping and saying "Ooh, Ooh" and trying to be on their best behaviour all at the same time. And there was Rooney, not knowing what to do for the best.

"Stop it! Stop it at once!" cried Aunt Tilda. No one knew who she was talking to. It could have been any one of them. She tried to pull them apart as though they were a bundle of straw with no feelings at all.

"Stop it, Tilda!" shouted Millie. "You will break our beads."

"Stop it, Tilda!" shouted Mollie. "You are pulling our hair."

"Stop it, Aunt Tilda!" shouted Rooney. "You are hurting my tail."

"Do something Walter," snapped Aunt Tilda, stamping her foot.

Pa wanted to laugh but he didn't dare. Will was hiding his face in the curtain trying to cover a smile that stretched from ear to ear.

"Keep absolutely still," said Pa.

"It's not easy when you are folded in half," said Mollie and Millie, from their folded up position.

"It's not easy when your tail is in a knot," said Rooney.

"Do as he says," snapped Aunt Tilda. So they did.

Carefully, very carefully indeed, Pa untangled Rooney's tail from the beads. As soon as he was free Rooney leapt into Will's outstretched arms and hid behind the curtain with him. That left Millie and Mollie still locked together by their hat pins but with their beads now dangling in long loops beneath their chins.

Carefully, very carefully, Pa drew out all the hatpins and handed them to Aunt Tilda.

Carefully, very carefully, Millie and Mollie stood up straight.

"What are you staring at?" they asked as Aunt Tilda's mouth began to twitch.

Aunt Tilda led them to the mirror.

"Oh my," said Millie and Mollie together, blushing the brightest red Rooney had ever seen. Their hats were perched on the tops of their heads like wrecked ships, and their hair usually so tidy, was in wisps round their faces. No one dared laugh because it would have offended Millie and Mollie and they had had quite enough to put up with for one day.

Aunt Tilda said she didn't think much of Rooney's best behaviour and he would have to do something to improve it. But Millie and Mollie said they quite understood about tails that had minds of their own, and it was their fault for tickling him.

The Measuring Stick

One morning Will was called to Doc West's house. He took Rooney with him. When they arrived, Doc West's sister showed them into the study.

"He's down there on the floor," she whispered as she closed the door behind them.

Doc was on his knees, grunting and groaning and grumbling. He was trying to reach something which was under the sofa. He turned round on his knees so that he was looking at Will's legs, and at Rooney's face.

"Can you get my pencil out from under there?" he said.

"If I have come all this way just to find a lost pencil I shall be cross," thought Will.

Rooney swept under the sofa with his tail. Out rolled the pencil, and three more with it. Doc put all four behind his ear and got to his feet.

"What can I do for you?" asked Doc as he brushed fluff from his knees.

"You mean, what can we do for you," said Will. "You sent for us, remember."

"So I did," said Doc. "I've got a problem I want you to fix."

He pointed to his writing table. It was covered with an untidy mess of papers and writing things.

"Every time I put a pencil down it rolls off the table and onto the floor," said Doc. "You can see how busy I am. I can't get on with my work when I have to keep chasing pencils. Sometimes I can't find them at all. I've lost five since Monday. I won't have any pencils left soon. Can you do something?"

"I'll show you what it does," said Doc. He banged his elbow on the edge of the table. The table wobbled and shook. The ink bottles rattled, papers began to slide.

24

Will walked round the table, twice, leaning on each side in turn as he went.

"One leg is shorter than the other three," said Will. "That is what is making it wobble. I'll make all the legs the same length."

"I'll hold the short leg for you," said Rooney.

Will couldn't see what good that would do but he knew Rooney wanted to help, so he said, "Hold it tightly then."

Rooney wrapped himself, and his tail, round the table leg as though he was a vine growing round a tree.

Doc swept all the papers into the armchair and put the ink bottles on the mantleshelf. Then Will turned the table upside down so that he could do the sawing. Before Rooney knew what was happening he was upside down too . . . AND sliding down the table leg. He didn't stop sliding until his head was touching the floor.

"Are you alright?" asked Doc.

"Think so," said Rooney. Everything looked so different when it was upside down.

"You can let go now," said Will. "Bring me the measuring stick please." The measuring stick wasn't in the tool bag. They had left it behind at the woodshed.

"I've got one somewhere," said Doc. "You can borrow mine if I can find it." He couldn't find it.

"I'll go back to the woodshed and get Will's," said Rooney.

"I know it's here somewhere," said Doc. He was on his knees looking under the sofa again. Rooney tried to squeeze past just as Doc began to move backwards. Doc couldn't see where he was going and

26

he didn't think to look. Rooney could see where he was going, but he couldn't move fast enough. If Will hadn't plucked Rooney into the air like a fish from a stream he would have been squashed.

Will was holding Rooney high in the air with his tail and his feet dangling. They were all laughing with relief at Rooney's narrow escape when Will suddenly said, "Stay just like that. Don't move anything. 'Specially don't move your tail."

"Why?" asked Rooney. "Is there something wrong with it?"

"Don't ask questions, just do it," said Will. So Rooney just did it and waited to see why he was just doing it.

Will knelt beside the table. He held Rooney so that his tail dangled beside the table leg. He moved him up, and then down again.

"I wonder what I'm doing," said Rooney to himself.

"Just as I thought," said Will. "We can use the rings on your tail as a measuring stick."

The short leg was twice as long as Rooney's tail with two more rings added on. The other legs were twice as long as Rooney's tail with three more rings added on. Will said that meant they had to measure one ring of Rooney's tail on each of the long legs and saw that much off.

Will measured. Doc made marks with his pencil. Then, while Will did the sawing Rooney and Doc went looking for other things to measure.

The sawing was finished. They were all banging their elbows on the table to test it for wobble when Pa came puffing through the door with the measuring stick.

"You left this behind," he said.

"We managed without it," laughed Will. "We have found a new way of measuring."

"Oh," said Pa. "Please explain what you mean."

They not only explained what they meant, they showed Pa what they meant.

"I never dreamed a tail could be so useful," said Pa.

Pa winked at Will. "I don't know how we will fit the new measuring stick into the tool bag," he said.

"Rooney will have to go into the tool bag with it," laughed Will.

"No, Rooney won't," laughed Rooney. "Rooney will carry it."